I0623462

SENTENCED TO LOVE

by Kathleen Morris

Amazon Edition
Copyright Kathleen Morris 2013
2nd Edition 2019

ISBN – 978-1-927828-46-5

Rouge Publishing 2019

DEDICATION
This story is dedicated to my mother who went through chemo and radiation like a superhero. Even though we lost you, cancer did not win!

SENTENCED TO LOVE

Claire Belafonte hadn't done a single reckless thing in her entire twenty-seven years of existence, except for this one time.

She could hear her mother's lifetime of warnings plague her not to pick up a hitchhiker, but today she didn't care. Today she wanted to mask the pain with any kind of danger she could find. It wasn't like she had anything to lose.

What was it all for anyway, this holding onto a hope that would never see the light of day? It was a life sentence and she knew what that meant. There were no lucky breaks for her, so why should she care what happened?

As the October drizzle mirrored her melancholy feelings, she slowed her brand-new Camero Z28 to a crawl and powered down the passenger window. A sudden panic rose in her chest as her heart pounded, *C'mon Claire, you can do this!*

"Need a ride?" she smiled like a silly woman who obviously hadn't done this before. Of course, he needed a ride, why else was he standing in the rain with his thumb out?

The man was drenched and shivering, and not what she'd expected. He was ruggedly handsome and looked like he hadn't slept in a week. His black stubble made his face look dirty and all he had to protect himself from the elements was a big orange garbage bag wrapped tightly around himself. Her cautious level-headed self would have forewarned her already and she never would've stopped in the first place. But not this time. This time she was bound and determined to do the opposite for a change and tempt fate instead. How much worse could it get anyway?

"Sure," the man said, opening the passenger door as he dropped inside.

"I'm Claire, and you are...?"

"Gavin."

As she eyed the hitchhiker, she suddenly felt a rush of anxiety. Had she really done it? Had she really picked up a stranger on the side of the highway? *What a fool!*

"You must be cold," she forced a conversation. "Forecast is for snow."

"Figures."

"Where're you headed?"

"North."

North didn't exactly tell her much but the man looked uncomfortable explaining himself. In fact, he looked downright miserable. As Claire pulled away from the shoulder and started to accelerate, she realized something was definitely wrong.

"I-I don't want to hurt you," he told her, suddenly pulling out a pistol. "Just do as I say and you won't get hurt."

"Okay-okay!" she gulped hard, shaking her head like she understood. This guy seemed serious, but for some reason, he didn't sound very threatening. What kind of a hijacker tells his victim he doesn't want to hurt her?

Silence ensued for quite a while with only the swish-swish sound of the windshield wipers working overtime. For miles, she listened to the rhythm until the sun started to set over the horizon. The steady rain had already turned to snow and visibility was getting near zero.

Claire was normally a nervous driver to begin with, without adding bad weather and kidnapping to the mix. It would be easy to pretend she couldn't handle the roads. But who'd be pretending? All she'd have to do is turn sharply and she'd spin out of control. But she'd likely die in the process or get herself shot before she could escape. Both were painful circumstances, and pain was what she was trying to avoid right now. She had far too much of that lately.

The self-defense class she enrolled in last year taught her to cause an accident if she was ever in a predicament like this, but it wasn't as easy as it sounded. She was traveling at a high speed, the roads were slippery, and she was in the middle of nowhere. Not exactly an ideal time to use one of Officer Dalton's wise escape techniques.

Then, from the corner of her eye, she noticed him lifting the orange bag, exposing a bloody sticky mess beneath. She gasped before she realized she did it out loud and turned quickly back to the road, steadying her gaze in front of her.

"Yeah *I'm shot*," Gavin barked as he pasted the plastic bag back on the wound, wincing in pain. "Just keep driving and stop looking at me like that.

"Like what?"

"Shocked."

"Well it's...*shocking.*"

The man just eyed her and shook his head without saying a word.

What was his problem anyway? Most people would be shocked seeing something like that, especially given the circumstances. She wondered if he shot himself with his own gun. She wouldn't be surprised.

If the roads weren't so bad, she could try and knock the gun out of his hand, but that would take skill and timing. No, for now she'd focus on her first priority: Driving. Besides, he was losing blood and getting weaker, and couldn't keep this up for long.

She hoped!

Claire wondered how many other unsuspecting people had picked up hitchhikers only to fall prey to something like this. It didn't pay to be a good Samaritan anymore. But was that what she was trying to do? If she wanted to do a good deed, she could have helped an old lady across the street, not this. No, she was on the run from her own life, and he just happened to provide the opportunity to do it.

It all came flooding back to her now, that smug look on the doctor's face when he told her the results this morning. There was no hope, no cure, just a death sentence, no matter what suggestions he made. Who did he think he was kidding? Certainly not her. The operation was absolutely out of the question.

But still, she didn't know which hurt more: the results; being told she needed surgery, or that stupid doctor with all the false hope he was dishing out like he was God. She knew the end result. She hadn't lived through the pain of losing her own mother to the very same disease for nothing. She learned the hard way that there was no cure even with the operation. It didn't add a single hour to her mother's life. No, she was done caring. Her vendetta against God was only just beginning. If He wanted to give her the same death sentence as her mother, she was going out kicking and screaming. Looking for danger was merely just part of it.

Even if the danger was sitting right next to her.

No, Claire was smart enough to realize she'd asked for this, but she hadn't anticipated just how dangerous it would be. "Playing with fire will always get you burnt," her mother would tell her numerous times as a child. And so be it. What was the alternative? Shriveling up into nothing and puking your guts out until your last dying day? No thanks! The fire was much more attractive, especially *this* fire.

Without warning, the low-gas indicator light came on and Claire realized she had to say something to the guy. "We need gas."

"Just keep driving."

"I can't," she snapped back. "We're almost empty, and cars don't run on air."

"*Fine!*"

"There's a town up ahead. I'll fill up there."

"Whatever," Gavin told her, wincing in pain as he tried to sit up straight.

"And you need a hospital."

"I *don't* need a hospital, it's just a graze."

Right! Claire knew a serious injury when she saw one. He was either going to pass out because of blood loss or get an infection, and she didn't want to be around to find out which one. Maybe if she was lucky, he'd leave her at the gas station, but not likely.

"After I fill up, you can take my car and leave me behind, okay?" she suggested, hoping he'd agree. But something told her it wasn't going to be easy to persuade him.

"Not okay. You're helping me get across the border.

"I beg your pardon?"

They were at least a couple days drive from the Canadian border and there was no way someone in his condition was getting through customs wearing an orange garbage bag covered in blood. She didn't have her passport anyway, and he likely didn't even own one.

"Just how am I gonna do that? And why would I help you anyway?"

"You're lonely and you need something," he whispered instead of shouting this time. "I can tell."

"I'm *not* lonely you jerk! Claire fumed. "And you don't even know me!"

"I know lonely."

With that, Claire bit her lip and didn't say another word. He was playing mind games with her and she needed time to think. Firstly, she *wasn't* lonely. *She wasn't!* She had friends and co-workers that cared about her a lot. They just didn't know she had terminal cancer yet. But when they find out, she was sure they'd care.

It was family she didn't have. Her father was out of the picture from day one, and her mother was the only family she ever had, up until a couple years ago. The two of them lived together in that small wartime house their whole lives. She was saving up for their dream home when her mother got sick. That's why she spent the money on her new car instead. What good was money if you didn't have anyone to spend it on. And the hopes of buying a dream home died that rainy Saturday along with her mother.

And there was no man for her. The one she was dating for a while turned out to be a train wreck. Most men in her life did. Absent father syndrome, her co-workers would say when she told them about her love life. They were repeats of her deadbeat dad, every single one of them.

So... *lonely?* Maybe she was. But right now, it was more than that. It was an unbelievable sorrow that seemed to crush her like a vice until she couldn't breathe. Something this jerk knew nothing about.

With the gas gage reading almost empty, and the yellow picture of a gas pump lighting up her dash, Claire knew she had to make a decision. The town of Hazen was coming up and though they didn't have much else there, they did have a gas station. Either she filled the car up or kept on driving until they ran out of gas. Both options made her cringe.

Perhaps she could escape at the gas station. It wouldn't be hard to just leave him there. After all, she had the upper hand with the car and a good pair of legs to run quickly. His bleeding wound wouldn't allow him to run after her for long.

But it was cold outside and a blizzard was brewing.

If she didn't bolt at the gas station and didn't fill the car, they'd run out of gas shortly and be stuck on the side of the road in a blizzard. He could do anything to her, and the gun would make it easy. No, she'd get the gas, play the game, and hope for a way to escape some other way. Preferably something that included her car so she didn't have to take off on foot in a frozen blizzard.

If she told the gas attendant to call the police, it might help the situation, but Claire wasn't sure what would happen if she did. He might still shoot her. She wiped her forehead and realized the town lights were peaking through the snow squalls. It was now or never.

"There's a town," Gavin said. "Take the next turn."

"And what if I don't?" Claire argued, deciding to play hardball.

"I'll have to shoot you then...*like I said!*"

Would he though? His eyes didn't really look mean. Was he a killer? Or was something else going on? What was his story anyway?"

"Fine! We get gas then," she fumed, turning sharply into the little town, going over train tracks a little too fast.

"Easy!"

She glared sideways at him and slowed down to a crawl.

The dark little town looked half asleep when she slowly rolled down the street. She knew where the gas station was, but it was still hard to find in the blinding snow. It wasn't like she spent a lot of time in Hazen, but she and her mother looked for houses there a few years ago thinking it would be nice to get out of the city.

They never found a single place for sale.

"I know it's around here somewhere," she squinted.

"Over there," Gavin pointed. "On the corner."
How helpful.

"Look," she said as she pulled the car to the side of the road and stopped short, "this can go two ways: One - either I'm forced to help you, or two - I do it on my own terms. I don't feel comfortable with that gun pointing in my face. And besides, you can't exactly follow me inside the gas station wearing that garbage bag, and I don't think you really wanna shoot me. So, how's this gonna go?"

Gavin dropped the gun and hung his head looking so pathetic Claire could hardly contain her sympathy. The man was obviously in turmoil over something, just like her. It pulled on her heartstrings even though she knew better. For some strange reason, she felt sorry for the man and found herself wanting to help.

"I can't do it!" Gavin finally spoke after a defeated moment of silence. He sighed heavily and breathed in a bout of pain, grabbing his injury. "I need your help, *please!*"

*

They had been on the road for hours now.

After filling up in Hazen they pushed toward the Canadian border. It was now well after midnight and the storm was only getting worse.

"We need to stop," Claire finally spoke, waking the man with a start.

"No," he groaned. "I told you I want to reach the border as soon as possible."

"I know that's what you *want,* but it's not what you *need.*"

"And who are you, *my mother?*"

"No, but I could be your friend if you let me." Claire was taking a risk with that statement, but she had to try to get through to him. He could fight her or let her help. Either way, they were stopping at the next town.

"Look, you asked for my help, so let me help you then. I need to take a look at that wound and clean it up. Be realistic, they won't let you near the border looking like that."

But the man just hung his head as if he were giving up, that, or he was losing his strength. Claire figured it was probably a little of both.

"What did you do anyway, rob a bank?"

"Something like that."

"Well, that doesn't exactly bode confidence. Either you did or you didn't?" She could tell she was frustrating him, but that was better than having him pass out. She had to keep him conscious if she was going to get him to a motel room.

Gavin didn't even bother to answer the question.

"Fine! Suit yourself. If you're not going to tell me what kind of trouble you're in, that's your business. But don't expect me to help you then."

Another manipulative tactic. Boy, she was good at this.

"All right! *Jeepers!* You don't give up do you?"

"Nope!"

"I busted out of the pen. *There,* you happy now? I escaped during transport. They were moving me to death row."

"For what?"

Silence stopped the conversation suddenly, leaving only the hum of the drive and the howl of the October wind.

"I-um...robbed an armored car."

"Seriously?" Claire knew they didn't give the death penalty to someone for that. But she'd let him get away with his lie for now. At least she got the adrenaline pumping through his veins. And just in time, the town of Clover was visible through the snow squall. They would be at a motel within minutes, and there she could dress his wounds and find out the *real* truth.

As the car came to a stop, Claire unbuckled her seatbelt and grabbed her purse. "Now, you stay here. Let me check us in and I'll come back and help you."

The man nodded.

A number of thoughts ran through her head, but the only one that stuck was, *Are you crazy, girl?*

Helping a fugitive was the farthest thing from sanity and she was okay with that for some strange reason. In fact, for the first time in a long time, she hadn't thought of her own hopeless case. For once the tragic circumstances were coming from someone else.

Believe it or not, that was a good thing.

"I'd like a room for the night," she told the front desk clerk as she handed him her credit card, bobbing her head back and forth to keep an eye on Gavin. He had better stay put if he knew what was good for him.

Look at her thinking like a fugitive with a totally different demeanor than a few hours earlier. Just thinking about it gave her a rush of adrenaline instead of self-pity. Twisted, but a welcome feeling none-the-less.

Inside the motel room, Claire helped Gavin to the closest bed and watched him ease onto it with a great deal of pain. She hoped she was able to clean his wound well enough to prevent infection. That thought sent her mind reeling.

"I need to go and get a few things," she told him.

"You're coming back though, aren't you?"

"Yes, I'm coming back."

The man sounded like a sick little boy who needed his mother. "I told you I'd help and I mean it. Besides, I'm not the kind of person who doesn't keep her word. In fact, I'm not the kind of person who does this either, but hey, better late than never."

She knew he didn't understand what she meant but that was okay, he didn't have to. He didn't seem to be coherent enough to understand much of anything right now. He just looked as though he was in a lot of pain.

Within a half hour, Claire returned with medical supplies she picked up from a nearby pharmacy. It wasn't exactly what she needed but it would have to do.

"Gavin, I'm back," she said, whispering into his ear. But his silence told her he was out cold. *Good time to work on him.*

Claire's nursing skills made treating the man a breeze and she was thankful for the ability to help him. Not many people could put twelve stitches in a guy with make-shift medical supplies from the dark ages.

"There," she spoke aloud, "that should do it. Now we wait."

Gavin moaned a bit as if he was trying to answer her, but his eyelids didn't open at all. The man needed to rest, and so did she.

As Claire curled up into a ball in her own double bed across the room from the stranger, she realized he was becoming more than just a stranger. He was a person who needed help. She still didn't know his story but for the most part, she didn't have to.

"Thank you," a week voice suddenly spoke in the darkness, interrupting her thoughts.

"You're welcome," she answered back, closing her eyes with a smile.

It had been so long since she felt like this. Approximately two years actually. She was her mother's sole caregiver, and the last two weeks of her life were awful. It seemed even with her nursing skills, she wasn't able to take the pain away. With a sigh, she hoped for sleep and pleasant dreams.

By morning, Claire woke up crying and she couldn't stop. All she could think about was her own prognosis. She felt her plump breasts and cried even harder.

"What's the matter?" a weak voice broke in.

But Claire just continued to cry into the sheets uncontrollably. It was as if all her pent-up emotions came bubbling to a head all at once and she couldn't stop.

"I won't hurt you!" the voice came louder, trying to sit up.

"No! Don't sit," she yelled. "*Please!* I don't want to have to stitch you back up again." But the man didn't listen. He managed to prop himself up to a half-sit on the bed.

"Why are you crying?"

"I don't knooow!"

But she knew. She knew that she was faced with the biggest challenge of her life. She knew she had to get the operation before the cancer spread. She knew either option meant death. If she got the operation, that would mean the end of her as a woman, and she'd rather die than do that. But, if she didn't get the operation, that meant she would die like her mother. Even if she got the operation, it didn't mean she'd live.

At this point, Claire decided life was over-rated anyway. She spent all day at work just to come home to an empty house. She ate, slept, and then did the same thing all over again. Sometimes she didn't even get home to sleep in her own bed with the back to back shifts she was taking at the nursing home lately. No, life was definitely over-rated.

"C'mere!" Gavin said, patting the spot on the bed beside him.

"No!"

"Look," he said, "I don't know you so you can tell me anything, so *please*, tell me what's wrong."

Claire stopped for a moment and looked up at the man. He had a compassionate look to his face and seemed to genuinely care. She decided to take him up on his offer and went over to sit on the end of his bed.

"Now, tell me why you're crying," he said. "You look sad and lonely and, in more pain, than I am."

Then Claire started to sob with great intensity.

"Come closer," Gavin insisted, motioning for her to move up.

Claire obeyed, but only because what he said was true. She *was* sad, she *was* lonely, and she *was* in pain. It was pathetic but she needed this destitute stranger somehow.

"Look," he handed her a Kleenex, "whenever my wife got like this, I just tickled her like this..."

Did he just tickle her?

"*Hey!*" Claire was getting mad now.

"And she usually got mad too," Gavin grinned.

"Do you mind? You don't even know me so get your hands off!"

But he ignored her and kept on tickling until Claire was spitting mad. "*Stop it!*"

"Not until *you* do!"

Claire was both crying and laughing at the same time, then suddenly, as if she realized his tactic had worked, she stared at him with understanding eyes. "Thank you," she gulped, hoping that was the end of her crying fit. "I don't know what got into me."

"Yes, you do," he said, "It's why you're here."

Silence.

Claire immediately got up and turned on the television for a distraction.

"I'm not done with you yet," he smirked. "Come back and sit down so we can talk."

Talk? She was scared to death of that.

With the droning of the weatherman in the background giving snow advisories for every region, she went back to Gavin and sat down.

"Look," he said, holding her hand in this time. He brushed her skin with his thumb in a compassionate gesture. "My wife suffered from depression. I know the signs, so please talk to me!"

Claire bit her lip and said nothing.

"I'll tickle you again."

"No, you won't."

"Will too."

Gavin reached to tickle her sides again but she pulled away quickly and smiled through her tears. "I have breast cancer."

An awkward silence paused their playful moment and Claire realized she had never even said the words out loud before.

"I'm sorry," he said will caring eyes.

It was embarrassing telling a perfect stranger something so personal, but for some reason, she felt she could tell him anything. It was an odd but welcome feeling.

"They want to chop off my breasts."

"So, let 'em!"

Claire's mouth hung open. "I beg your pardon?"

"You heard me," he repeated. "*Let 'em!*"

Claire was insulted. Who did he think he was, telling her to do something like that? How could he flippantly give her such serious advice? Did he even know how that would affect her?

"That's easy for you to say! My *boobs* are all I have! I'm not pretty like everyone else. All I have are these *double D's!*"

"So, you'd rather die?"

"No!"

"Well then..."

"I'll have you know that breast cancer *is* a death sentence! Even if I get the operation, I'll still die from it."

"That's a load of crap!"

"It's *true!*"

"No, it's not Claire! You don't know the future. I'm the one that's dying. Death row is a *real* life sentence. At least you have a fighting chance and that's all I've ever wanted."

"And you call what you're doing a fighting chance?" Claire spit back. She knew she was throwing it back in his face, but he was wrong. She had a death sentence same as him.

"It's the best I can do," Gavin frowned.

"And this is the best *I* can do."

They were at a standstill. Why was she even arguing with the man? He couldn't possibly understand. What did he know anyway?

"We're both running Claire." And that was her answer. He knew all too well.

"I know."

"C'mere," he opened his arms to her.

"No!"

And then he pulled her to him, kissing her softly on the lips.

"There," he smirked, "you're beautiful, and not because of those double D's, but because you helped me have a fighting chance."

Claire felt her heart skip a beat. The kiss was warm and gentle and she realized she was connected to this man in more ways than one. In all her years of dating, she had never once felt like this.

"I thought you were married. Why'd you kiss me if you have a wife?"

"*Had* a wife - she died."

"Oh."

"It's fine."

But he didn't look fine. His stubble jaw shifted as he tried to fight off tears.

"What happened?"

Gavin shook his head, not saying anything for a minute, then cleared his throat. "She was...*sick.*"

Claire grabbed his hand with both of hers, hoping he'd elaborate. It was none of her business how she died, but curiosity got the best of her. "Cancer?"

"No - mental illness."

"*Oh!*"

"Yeah, that's the usual response."

"I'm sorry," Claire apologized. "I didn't mean..."

"You didn't have to."

Silence.

Dumb! Why did she have to say it like that?

Claire felt awful. She didn't understand mental illness, even though she'd seen it first hand in the care home she worked at. Dementia and depression especially. Alzheimer's was the worst. But mental illness wasn't exactly an easy sickness to understand. In fact, most of the time people used the term too loosely. In her opinion, it was usually used as an excuse for bad behavior.

If truth be told she didn't really believe in mental illness, as bad as that sounded. Didn't everyone suffer from depression of some kind or another? Everybody struggled, had good days and bad days, and there was no such thing as normal.

Claire left Gavin pouting on the bed, and set off across the room to the window, pulling the curtains open. It was still snowing.

A certain melancholy hung over her as she looked at the vehicles covered with snow in the parking lot. Not a soul ventured out; only the dull mumble of the television filled the room with background noise. Maybe she'd better turn it up to get a weather report, she decided, grabbing the remote from the nearby table.

Five more inches of snow expected. *Great!*

"I'm sorry Claire," came a voice from the bed suddenly. It was Gavin with a change of face.

"Hmmm?"

"I said I'm sorry."

"I should be the one that's sorry. It's none of my business."

"But I want you to know," he insisted. "My wife had...*bipolar.*"

Claire was surprised. Bipolar wasn't something people talked about. There was a terrible stigma attached. Still, she was skeptical about the so-called disease especially when everyone acted a little bit bipolar sometimes. But she supposed she could be wrong. As she said, she didn't understand mental illness. All she could say was, "I see."

Gavin looked at her funny and continued.

"She really struggled with it," he told her. "It was *hard.* She'd be normal one minute, and then all of a sudden, she'd be crazy. She had type two. They called it *rapid cycle.* It was hard to know exactly what I was coming home to every day. *Really,* if you know anyone that has to go through this, it's total stress both for those diagnosed with it and those that love the ones that have it. Nobody really understands unless they've been through it."

"Okay..." Claire answered with an unsure tone. Really, she'd never heard of the type two kind. So many people used it as an excuse for their spouse's bad behavior when really, they were just spoiled adults who lacked discipline. But maybe she shouldn't be so judgemental.

"I know what you're thinking," he said. "But really, mental illness is just as painful as any physical illness. People don't take you seriously unless you have cancer. Don't get me wrong, cancer is horrible, but so is mental illness. It took me years to get a doctor to recognize she needed help. And finally, when they did...it was too late."

"What happened?" Claire asked, wondering if she even wanted to know.

"She - um - *it was too late.*"

"What do you mean, too late?"

"I lost my family."

"*What?*"

Claire was interrupted by a news bulletin then, stopping their discussion mid-sentence. She turned to listen. "*Convicted child killer, Gavin Parker Stevenson escaped custody yesterday while in transport from court proceedings that sentenced him to the death penalty for killing his four children and wife, two years ago,*" the reporter went on.

Claire gasped.

"*Stevenson is armed and dangerous and under no circumstances is he to be approached. Please call 911 immediately if you know the whereabouts of this man.*"

A mug shot of Gavin flashed across the TV screen.

Claire spun on her heels, "*A murderer? You killed your family?*"

"*No!*" Gavin protested.

"GET AWAY FROM ME YOU PIG!"

Claire backed up all the way to the wall and hit it with a thump as the murdering lunatic inched forward with his hands out.

"*Please!* I didn't kill them!"

"You LIAR!"

"Let me explain!"

"Explain? How, by lying to my face? I TRUSTED YOU!"

Gavin had her pinned against the wall with his muscular arms, grabbing both shoulders hard.

"LET ME GO!"

"*Not until you listen!*"

"I don't wanna listen to any more lies!"

"*They're not lies!*"

But Claire screamed *'HELP'* which made Gavin cover her mouth and force her to be quiet. "I don't want to hurt you but you gotta listen to me. I didn't kill my family, *please!* I'll explain everything but just give me a chance. Promise me you'll be quiet and I'll let you go."

His hand was hurting her mouth, and she could barely breathe. All she could do was whimper muffling sounds with wide eyes of panic.

Think Claire, think!

"Are you gonna be quiet?"

Claire shook yes, and just as he removed his hand, she made her move. *Pow!* Right to the groin with a knee. Then a quick fist to the stitches did him in, sending him careening to the floor in pain. Her self-defense classes paid off.

Gavin lay there in the fetal position moaning.

Claire contemplated her next move and looked around for something to tie his hands and feet with. Quickly she grabbed the Venetian blind strings and yanked.

Hurry up girl, she told herself as she fumbled to tie him up as quickly as her shaky hands would let her.

"Now try to get out of that you son-of-a..."

"Claire...*stop!*"

"I'll gag you like you did me if you don't shut up!"

Silence.

As she wiped her sweaty brow, she finished her knots and caught her breath. He wasn't going anywhere. Now all she had to do was grab the phone and call 911. They'd have him back in custody in no time. Thankfully she saw the news bulleting in time. She could only imagine what he had planned to do with her. And kissing him was a distant memory. How could she be so stupid and naive anyway?

"*Please* Claire! Listen to me!" Gavin desperately pleaded as she grabbed the phone, about to punch in the numbers.

"I told you to shut up!"

But Gavin moaned and began bashing his head over and over against the floor. His insanity was beginning to show with his childish tantrum.

"*I didn't do it!*" he cried."*I didn't do it! Why doesn't anyone believe me?!*"

While Claire observed his behavior, something tortured her inside. How pathetic he looked bound up, bashing his head against the floor bawling like a child. Perhaps she should hear him out?

Suddenly Gavin stopped and lay still, sobbing now in a low whimper. She decided to set the phone down to observe him for a few minutes. After all, she needed to see if he was okay. She wasn't a monster like him and didn't want to be responsible for someone's death even if he was a child killer. Calling the police could surely wait a few minutes.

"Gavin?" she called as she kneeled beside his bloody head.

He didn't answer.

Claire sat there on her knees looking at the man. He continued to sob and she wondered what to do. It was her nature to help, but this was too much. She had already helped him and he lied to her. Why should she be sympathetic?

"Fine then," she sighed, biting her lip, "I'll listen."

But Gavin ignored her.

"I said I'll listen."

Silence.

He was bleeding from his torn open stitches and from his head. He was in pain, but obviously conscious. Maybe she could at least make him comfortable. She went to the bed and grabbed a pillow and blanket, lifting his head while sliding the pillow underneath.

Still, he lay there motionless like some injured animal.

Next, she went to the bathroom and ran warm water over a white facecloth and rung it out, kneeling again beside him. She gently washed away the bloodstreams that were running down the sides of his head and cleaned around his forehead and eyes. For a moment, she saw a little boy in that manly unshaven face that had given up on himself and the rest of the world. The defeat was the only thing she recognized. Kind of like her own situation and that flooded her emotions with unspeakable pity.

"Are you okay Gavin?" she asked softly, wiping his forehead.

He wouldn't even open his eyes.

She saw this kind of behavior in the nursing home many times and it was very difficult to deal with. When an elderly patient gave up, there was little they could do but wait it out. Claire didn't have time to wait it out, so she decided to take things into her own hands. She'd force him to speak.

With a pop, she set back on her heals grabbing some towels, another blanket, and a pillow. She bent over, laying the blanket out for a makeshift bed for herself right alongside Gavin. If he wouldn't talk to her, she'd lay right beside him until he opened his eyes.

"For what it's worth," she whispered, staring at his closed eyes, "I'm sorry." Hopefully, he'd forgive her but all he did was wince when she shoved the towel against his belly. "This will stop the bleeding for now."

Gavin fluttered his eyelids and drew in a long breath. A tear gently streamed down the corner of his eye, dribbling into his mouth.

"Tell me what happened."

"It doesn't matter now."

"Yes, it does."

But when he opened his blue eyes, she realized they were the window to his wounded soul, and they were telling her that he was no murderer. But still, she needed some answers.

"How did your family die?"

A pain so visible, washed across his face when he spoke. "She did it."

"What do you mean, she did it?"

"My wife," Gavin choked, "I-I walked in on it."

An unimaginable horror, struck Claire as she realized what he was saying. The tears started to freefall from his tender eyes once more.

"Our twin girls were only a couple months old," he swallowed, licking the tears. They were the youngest. The boys loved their sisters but all they did was cry. It was hard on my wife, especially with the bipolar. She wanted to go off her meds while she was pregnant, and that was a nightmare. I thought she'd go back on after the girls were born but she wanted to stay off to breastfeed."

Claire listened as she held his hands. She guessed she could untie them now, but figured she'd do it later so she didn't interrupt him.

"Of course - Go on."

"But she couldn't handle the colic. I should have known better than to go back to work when I did. But we had bills to pay and I wanted some relief from the constant crying too. I was selfish. I should have stayed."

"No... *I understand.*"

But Gavin was shaking his head; Tears flooding his eyes. "I called the doctor, but he didn't listen to me. He told me to force her back on the meds, but she wouldn't. My wife was stubborn. She didn't let anyone force her to do anything, not even me. She wanted to breastfeed and that was that. I couldn't get her mind off of it, and she wouldn't do both, even if me and the boys were suffering because of her mood swings."

Claire just frowned and looked into his sad eyes. *This man was no murderer.*

"Then, I got a frantic call at work one day. My wife sounded like a crazy person. She screamed in my ear, told me she needed me to come home because she'd done something unforgivable. I rushed home immediately and...." Gavin broke out sobbing. He didn't have to tell her anymore, she already knew. Claire gulped back the tears and pressed her forehead to his.

"*She killed my babies Claire*...and then I tried to grab the knife from her. It didn't matter though. She deliberately threw herself from the second-floor banister and landed on the glass coffee table below. Glass went through her and she died instantly. When the police arrived, I had blood on my hands and my fingerprints on the knife. I was taken into custody. I wasn't even able to go to their funeral."

The man cried like a baby. He was in such excruciating pain telling the story she didn't know how to comfort him except to kiss his trembling lips. For a long moment, they lingered there as if it would heal the sorrow.

"I'm sorry," she finally broke.

And then he kissed her again with passion.

Finally, Claire pulled herself back and cleared her throat. "I have to stitch you up again, and then we need to get you out of here."

After a long afternoon of stitches and cleanup, they were both ready to go when the motel manager knocked on the door. Without thinking, Claire opened it.

"Oh hi," he said, peering into the room.

She hoped he hadn't recognized Gavin. What was she thinking opening the door so quickly? Gavin turned away from the man in a hurry.

" I thought you were staying another night since you stayed passed checkout."

"No, just one night like I said."

The man looked alarmed when he saw the bloody towels in a heap on the floor. "I got some complaints about a fight earlier. Are you okay?

"We're fine," she told him as she tried to close the door.

"Okay then," the motel manager sighed, "but I'll have to charge you for another night because you stayed past checkout - *and for damages.*"

"Fine then," she frowned, pulling two hundred dollars from her purse. She hoped it was enough.

Once he was gone, she rested against the closed door. "That was close? Do you think he recognized you?"

"I don't know, but I don't want to find out. Let's get out of here!"

Claire helped Gavin shuffle to the car, but he couldn't move very fast with his injuries. She looked around but nobody was outside in the storm to see them leave. It was crazy to head back on the icy roads, but they didn't exactly have a choice.

She contemplated her actions again but realized she was in this for the long haul now. Gavin was no murderer; she knew that now. And he was more than a friend. Her attraction to him had taken her off guard because it was stronger than anything she'd ever felt before.

All she knew was they had to get out of there and fast.

"I hope you have a plan Gavin," she told him, "because you're gonna need a good one to get through the border without a passport."

"Who says I need a passport? I was born in Canada so I'm a Canadian citizen. Do you know how many people get across the border without proper documentation? About three thousand, daily. Seriously, all I need is a believable story. And once

I get into Canada, I'll be home free. I have no record there, and they don't have a reason to arrest me. I've done nothing criminally wrong there."

"You've done nothing criminally wrong *here*."

"Yeah well...tell that to my lawyer. He never believed my story for one minute. Said all the evidence pointed to me. Well yeah...can't argue with that now can you."

"Yes, *you can!*"

"Don't you think I tried Claire? I tried everything. It was hopeless. You heard what the media called me: *A child killer*."

"I know," she frowned, focussing on the icy road ahead. The snow had ended but the highway conditions were critical.

The car slipped, twisted, and turned sideways at one point.

"Do you want me to drive?"

"Can you? I mean, do you feel up to it? Because I don't want to end up in the ditch. I've never been good at driving in these conditions. Actually, I suck, don't I?"

"Yeah, pretty much," he laughed.

It was good to see him smile; It was a contagious one. The two of them met each other's eyes and then Claire blushed and turned back to the road. "I'll pull over."

As she stopped and got out, she stretched and breathed in the cool crisp air. The pungent smell of wet leaves and the trees in the background made for a picturesque view, even though it was getting dark. It was almost suppertime and she realized she was famished.

Gavin stood in the snow now, inhaling deeply. "Smell that?" he said. "That's the smell of the wild. I always told my boys that when I took them hunting around this time of year. Took my oldest one out for the first time when he was only two and a half. Can you believe that? All he did was watch his daddy with big bug eyes like I was a superhero."

"Bet you were a good dad."

"Hope so."

"How old were your boys?"

"Five and three."

Claire quickly tried to change the subject before she lost Gavin in his painful memories again. She scooped up a handful of wet snow and formed a ball.

"Oh no you're not," he grinned, scooping up some for himself.

The two of them threw snowballs at each other, missing each other and laughing as they danced around the car. Gavin shuffled.

"Hey now, that's not fair. I can barely move."

"*Ah-ha!*" she teased, "that just gives me an advantage."

"Okay smarty pants, *take that!*"

A snowball hit Claire square in the middle of her forehead. She screamed and darted away. "Oh, you're dead meat!" She wiped her eyes and mouth clear and raked her hands through the snow again, throwing yet another one - but missing him by a mile.

"Oh, so driving isn't the only thing you suck at."

"Shut up," she laughed, trying to throw another snowball only to have him take it from her hand before she had a chance to throw it.

"*You bugger!*"

Gavin pinned her against the car, falling toward her more than anything. "Ouch," he groaned, "that hurt."

"Serves you right!"

"Oh yeah?"

"Yeah!"

They were both breathing heavy against each other as Gavin met her eyes. "I don't know what it is about you, but you make me feel so...*alive!*"

"Me too."

"Well alive is a good thing," he told her as he held her tight, "especially since this is the first time, I've actually felt *alive* in a long time. Sure beats the alternative."

Claire hung her head then, remembering what drove her to pick him up in the first place. She didn't want to remember.

"Hey," he lifted her chin with his hand. "What's the matter?"

"Nothing."

But Gavin wouldn't take that for an answer. He was too wise for his own good. It was as if he could see right through her.

"Get the operation Claire - *Live!*"

And before she could say a word, his mouth covered hers with passion. She could taste his cold lips, and the peanut butter granola bar he ate earlier.

Breathe!

It lasted longer than Claire expected and broke only because she had no more air. They held each other for a moment, forehead to forehead. "What are we doing Gavin?"

"What do you mean?"

"*This* - You and me."

Then Gavin withdrew and backed away from her. "You're right," he frowned. "We can't do this. I- I don't want to hurt you."

With that, they both got back in the vehicle and took off into the late afternoon. Gavin drove like a pro, and his confidence behind the wheel put her at ease, at least for the time being. All she could think of was the kiss, but it would be wrong to encourage him even though her heart was still pounding. There were other more important things going on but she didn't want to think about them now, though she probably should.

It wasn't just the thought of having surgery for a double mastectomy that scared her, it was the thought that it wouldn't make any difference at all, like what happened with her mother. It was the fact that she wouldn't feel like a woman anymore, or be able to have kids. Not that she ever thought she'd have kids, but hearing Gavin talk about his, made her think of the possibilities.

If she had met Gavin years ago, before he had his own family, maybe the two of them would've had a chance together. But it was too late now. They had both run out of time. It was hopeless. How was she supposed to choose life when there was no more life left?

But she didn't want to think about it anymore. Instead, she curled up in a ball and let the sway of the vehicle rock her to sleep. Maybe this was all a bad dream and she'd wake up happy, healthy, and in love? *In another lifetime perhaps.*

"Wake up sleeping beauty," the voice startled Claire. It was her fugitive again, but now he was driving through traffic.

"Where are we?"

"Verdock. We're about two hours from the border."

"I'm starving."

"Me too. Guess we should stop for food. I hate to beg you for money but..."

"Oh, no problem. Let me get my purse."

She could tell he was embarrassed. Most guys generally liked to pay and make it known that they had money. She assumed Gavin was no exception. It must be hard for him to depend upon her.

"Look, I said I'd help and that means with my money too. I don't mind."

"I know you don't mind, but that doesn't mean I have to like it. I had a good paying job before they locked me up. I'm used to being the provider."

"What did you do?"

"Computer programmer."

"I see. That kind of a guy, hey?"

"What kind of a guy?"

"A nerd," she winked.

"Hey, I'm not a nerd. I programmed stuff for NASA I'll have you know."

"My point exactly: *A Nerd!*"

"Whatever, *smarty pants*," he chuckled, taking her teasing lightly as he tried to play along with her. In fact, he was more easygoing than any guy she'd ever met. That was a charming quality in itself.

"There's a McDonald's over there," she pointed.

"Ew, you like that crap?"

"Love it!"

"Whatever," he shook his head and laughed. "I guess we're going to McDonald's then. Drive-thru or go inside?"

"Well unless you want the whole world to recognize you, I think we'd better go through the drive-thru."

"But they can still see my face as I drive through."

"Right, didn't think of that. Guess I'm going inside by myself."

Gavin pulled into the dark parking lot and brought the car to a stop. "Don't mind me, I'll just wait here in the car like a little kid."

"Oh, *Gavin.* You're not a little kid, you just need help."

"I know, and I hate it!"

She blew a teasing kiss and headed into the McDonalds. Once she got inside, she saw a group of people gathered around a wall-mounted television. It was broadcasting a news bulletin with her picture on it saying she was abducted by the escaped child killer.

Whaaat? How did they know she was with him?

The motel manager must have blabbed. What a jerk. He must have seen Gavin after all. That meant they were looking for her car and tracking her credit card transactions. Suddenly panic washed over her face as she ducked into the bathroom and sat in the stall, breathing heavily. What were they going to do now?

Calm down, girl!

An idea came to mind. She'd pulled her loose black hair into a ponytail, put her hood up, and decided to paint her face. Goth was best. They wouldn't be able to recognize her then. She got her black eyeliner and compact mirror out and sat there on the toilet. She painted her lips black and smacked them together. Then she smeared black on her eyelids, drew a tear at the corner of each eye, and drew stitches on one side of her face.

Goth. *There!*

Finally, she took a stick of gum from her purse and started chewing. It was the best disguise she could think on short notice. And she was definitely still getting food. They were both too hungry for her to walk out of the restaurant without buying anything to eat.

As she left the stall, she paused in front of the mirror for a moment, unable to recognize herself. It was as if some stranger was warning her to stop this nonsense and call the police immediately. But she couldn't - she wouldn't.

"I'll have two Big Mac meals and supersize the fries please," she told the cashier. Then she used cash to pay and took off as fast as she could.

Gavin was startled when she slid back into the passenger seat. "What did you do to your face?"

"I know," she frowned. "Pretty bad eh?"

"*Scary!* I gather they posted your picture along with mine?"

"You got it."

Gavin put the car into gear and sped off into the night. They had decided they'd park in an alley somewhere and eat since they were both so hungry. That would give them time to figure out what to do next. They gobbled their food like ravenous wolves in complete silence.

"Look," Gavin mumbled with his last mouthful, "you don't have to do this. I can leave you at the nearest payphone. You can call the police and be home in your own bed tonight. Really, this is too much to ask."

"No, I can't," she wiped her mouth with a serviette, still chomping. "I had many chances to run, but I can't leave you now. It's not right!"

Gavin sighed and raked his fingers through his hair. "We can't take the car then. They obviously know we're traveling in it. It's no wonder they haven't spotted us by now. It's only a matter of time."

"I say we keep going," she insisted. "If they haven't found us yet, we have a shot at the border. We'll hide the car somewhere before we get there and then we'll walk across. It's been done before. We'll say the car was stolen and so was our I.D. We can do this!"

"We? There is no 'we' remember? I can't let you ruin your life, Claire."

"Ruin my life? How can it possibly be ruined any more than it already is?"

Silence.

Claire knew he was considering her idea, and figured they'd have a fighting chance if they hurried. It wasn't far to the border. All they had to do was fill up with gas and they'd be on their way.

"Okay, we go for it," Gavin finally decided, "but we do it my way. First, we have to stop for gas and get a few things."

"What things?"

"Just things. And you can use the restroom and take that black stuff off your face."

"Why?"

"Because Claire," he frowned. "If we get caught, they might charge you for aiding and abetting if they think you were helping me. The makeup makes you look like you didn't want to be found."

"Well, I don't."

"I know," Gavin sighed. "But seriously, this might not end well."

She didn't want to think about that. All she wanted to do was get the gas and get the heck out of there.

As they pulled into a corner self-serve gas station, Claire filled the car while Gavin slouched below the dash. Then, she went inside and purchased the gas with cash, along with some plastic zip ties about twelve inches long. She had no idea why he wanted them but did what she was told. Obviously, he had a plan that he wasn't sharing.

Next, she used the bathroom and washed off the black makeup with soap and water, left her ponytail in, and snuck out with her hood up. Nobody saw her leave.

"Okay, I did what you said," Claire told him when she returned.

"Let's see."

Claire held up the bag of zip ties.

"Good girl, now open the package and take some out."

Claire obeyed as Gavin ripped out of the parking lot, drove down the deserted street and stopped short alongside the service road at the edge of town.

"What are you doing?" she asked nervously.

"You'll see."

Gavin got out of the vehicle and went around to her side, opening the door. He buckled her in tightly and asked for the zip ties?

"Here," she trembled. She had no idea what he was up to, but something in the pit of her stomach warned her not to trust him. He quickly grabbed her wrists and pulled them together, zipping the ties tight.

"*No!* What are you doing?"

"It's for your own good!"

Panic and anger consumed her at the same time. "Stop it! *Stop it!*"

He grabbed her ankles while she wiggled and screamed but he had them zipped in a hurry, and then slammed the passenger door shut. If this was his kind of a joke, she didn't find it funny at all. But something told her it was no joke.

Had she been wrong about this man? *Apparently!*

Gavin got back in the driver's seat and sped off toward the highway without saying a word. He looked mad and unapproachable, but it was time for answers, and he better darn well give them to her. "What are you doing?"

"In case you didn't realize *Claire*, you're supposed to be my prisoner. If they catch us, you'll be thanking me that I tied you up. I don't want them to mistake you for my partner. Okay?"

"Oh." She guessed he was right, but it wasn't exactly the way she pictured them fleeing to the border. Her idea didn't include restraints. She questioned his reasons but wouldn't make an issue of it. He seemed genuine enough. *She hoped!*

"Seriously, you don't want to go to prison Claire," he went on. "If anything happens, you tell them I kidnapped you. Do you hear? You tell them you were held against your will and I made you do *everything!*"

"Okay...*I guess.*"

"*I mean it!* You don't tell them you helped me! Do you understand?"

"I understand. But why are you being so crazy?"

"Because Claire," Gavin worked his jaw and accelerated faster. "Two cop cars drove by when you were inside the gas station, that's why."

"Really?"

"Yeah, so they're looking."

A silence fell over them then, as they continued down the icy highway. She hoped the police hadn't noticed her car, and Gavin was just paranoid. For a while he said nothing, and after an hour went by and nobody followed, Gavin started to relax again.

"I'm sorry Claire," he started. "I didn't mean to scare you. I just want you to be safe. You don't know what it's like in jail. I was locked up with hardcore criminals for the last two years and - well - you don't wanna know what they do. Women's prisons are pretty much the same, just a different gender. I don't want you to go to jail for me."

"I know," Claire frowned. "I don't blame you. I just didn't expect you to tie me up. How am I supposed to run to the border like this?"

"When the time comes," he told her, "we'll hide the car in the country somewhere and I'll take your leg ties off. I'll use the pocket knife I found in your glove compartment to cut them off, so don't worry. You might be surprised what you find in your glove compartment, just like the granola bars."

Claire had to laugh at that. He was right. She didn't really know all the stuff she kept in her car. At least they had something to cut the ties with and that made her breathe a little easier.

"Your wrists stay tied until we get to the border. Just in case you know. I'll feel better that we left them on if they catch us. When I feel it's safe, I'll cut them off too. But not until then. We'll leave the gun and the knife somewhere, then we go across the border with nothing, just like we planned. We were robbed, our car was stolen along with our passports. You pretend to be my wife, and you let me do the talking."

"But they know our faces."

"*Rats!* I forgot that."

"I told you I should've stayed Goth."

"*Please* - No!" he grinned.

They both laughed. He was returning to his old self again. But they had to come up with some kind of disguise if this was going to work. "My Goth face wasn't that bad was it?"

"Yes! It was! Besides, you're much prettier as yourself."

"You think I'm pretty?"

That made her beam. She'd been called many things before but pretty was never one of them. Her boyish square jaw and boring black hair never brought male attention before. And her short stocky build definitely didn't bring the looks. It was usually only the double 'D's that brought the attention and that was it.

"Of course," Gavin smiled, "you're gorgeous!"

"Hmmm, you're not just saying that because of my double 'D's, are you?"

"What? *No!*" he said. "You're obsessed over those things, aren't you?"

"*No!*"

"Boobs are overrated," he smirked. "Seriously! My wife - well, let's just say breastfeeding kind of changes your perception. There are many other features on a woman that make her beautiful. And I'm not just talking about looks. I'm talking about what's inside. *Her heart.* You have a good heart, Claire."

"*Wow!* No guy has ever said that to me before. *I'm stunned.*"

"Well, then they were all idiots!"

You got that right.

"I grew up thinking my boobs were my best feature."

"Well they aren't," he told her flat out, "now get rid of them."

"Oh, just like that?"

"Yeah, just like that."

He had the nerve, telling her *that* out of the blue. He had no idea what he was talking about, and frankly no right to be talking to her about *that* at all.

"Easy for you to say."

"It's do or die, Clair, now that's your double 'D'."

Cleaver!

He knew she didn't want to talk about this yet he kept pushing her. *Do or die?* Bet he thought he was pretty smart for coming up with that one.

"I could say the same for you, Mr. Death Row."

"What's that supposed to mean?"

"Well - this is *your* do or die, isn't it? *I'm* - your do or die"

He was quiet for a moment. Claire could see the wheels turning. He was trying for a comeback and he was the type that could pull it off successfully. Not like her.

Here it comes.

"Well, you're exactly right," he told her seriously. "I just spent the last two years with murderers, and rapists, and child molesters, and now I'm told I'll be put to death for something I didn't even do. This escape thing I'm doing - at least I'm fighting. At least I *want* to live. Either I do this, or I die. So yeah, you're my double 'D' if you want to put it that way. You on the other hand - you don't even know what you've got. You *have* a life. You *have* a chance. You told me either you get the operation or you die. Well - do or die, baby. You can't have both. You don't *need* both. Take it from me. *Fight like hell!*"

That made her cry. It wasn't fair; it wasn't right to talk to her that way, but he was right. *He was exactly right.* Still, he crossed the line. It was a private matter and he needed to respect that it was her decision not his, and he couldn't bully her into it. "I'm not getting the stupid operation so just *stop!*"

"I'm not going to stop Claire!" he snapped back. "You need to listen to *someone!* If my wife would have listened to me when I told her to stay on her meds, *this* wouldn't have happened at all. I would still have my life...*my kids.*"

"Well, I'm *not* your wife."

"No, but if you were, I'd drag you kicking and screaming into that operating room and I wouldn't think twice."

She turned to the window and let the tears fall. He had no right to judge her. Who was he anyway? Just some guy who didn't know anything about her struggles; Just some screw up who thought he had the right to tell her what was best for her; Just some guy she was...*falling in love with.*

Always the wrong guy Claire, always the wrong guy!

She sniffled and turned to him again. "Okay, I've got something for you," she fumed. "If I was *your* wife, I never would have wanted to get pregnant in the first place. I wouldn't have gone off my meds, and I never would have.... *never would have...*"

She couldn't even say it.

"Killed them?"

She shook her head in shame.

"Look, Claire," he frowned, "I know what you're trying to do but it won't work. If something happens and I don't make it, promise me you'll try. Promise me you'll give yourself a fighting chance...*for me - for yourself.* You deserve that. Get the operation; beat the cancer; find a good man and settle down with a couple kids. *Be happy!* God knows that's all I ever wanted. *Seriously,* maybe it really is about the double 'D's as stupid as that sounds. Do it or die."

But she sat silent.

She didn't want to fight. She'd watched her mother fight so hard it tore her heart out. And in the end, it didn't make any difference at all. She still died a painful death. No, she didn't want *that*. She didn't even want to settle down and have a couple kids. Why should she? Just so they could watch *their* mother die? And she definitely didn't want to find a good man; there were none left. All she wanted was the man she couldn't have. All she wanted *was him!*

Suddenly, Gavin gripped the steering wheel and slowed down. "What's *that?*"

"What?"

"Those lights in the distance?"

Claire saw it too. "Is that what I think it is?"

"Yup! Roadblock."

"Now what?"

Gavin shifted the Camaro Z28 into neutral and turned off the engine. "The last thing we want is for them to see us coming."

"Maybe they already did."

"I hope not," he said, pounding the steering wheel. "*Stupid!* I should've known they'd do this."

"Can we go around?"

"I don't know," Gavin chewed his lip, thinking. "What we need is to drive with the lights off but these stupid new cars don't let you do that."

"Mine does," she told him. "It has a switch kit in the dash."

"Seriously? What switch?"

"That red one to your left"

Gavin flicked it down immediately and then brought the engine to life. No lights. She hadn't even tried it before, but thankfully it worked. They were running in the dark now. With a thrust of the gear shifter, Gavin forced it into reverse as he stepped on the clutch at the same time. They sped backward on the ice and did a complete turnaround. He braked, stepped on the clutch again, and shifted into first, bringing up the gears as he increased speed in the opposite direction. Claire was glad he was so familiar with a standard transmission. She was still learning, and wouldn't have been half as fast. "What do we do now?"

"*We run!*"

Of course! That was a silly question. Running blind in the dark with no lights in a snowstorm was a crazy combination, but she couldn't think of anyone else she'd rather have behind the wheel. Surely, he must have been a race car driver in another lifetime. He forced her Camaro into speeds she had never taken it before. It knocked her body around like a rag doll, forcing her to grab on with her zip-tied hands. He found a gravel road and took a sharp left off the highway, booting it down to the end in seconds. Then another road, and another one until they were out in the middle of nowhere.

He nervously checked the rear-view mirror every step of the way.

"Could we leave the car somewhere?" she asked.

"I don't know."

Gavin was thinking again. It was almost midnight and they were so close to the border they could taste it. Unfortunately, the police probably had barricades everywhere.

"We need a map," Gavin said quickly. "Do you have one?"

"I don't carry paper maps. I use the GPS on my cell phone but it died sometime last night. Sorry."

"Does the car have GPS?"

"Didn't want the bells and whistles."

Gavin groaned. He stopped the vehicle and shifted into neutral, letting the rumbling engine idle. "We have to wait it out then."

"What do you mean?"

"Well, we're boxed in. They have everything blocked off, and we have no way to know where we are for sure. If we're gonna leave the car somewhere it has to be at least within walking distance of the border. And the cops are crawling everywhere. It's too dangerous now. Our best bet is to go back to town and sit tight. Maybe in a few days, they'll take down the roadblocks and think we headed somewhere else. Then, when they're not expecting it, we'll cross the border. Plus, that'll give us time to come up with a proper disguise for both of us."

"I guess."

"This isn't a game you know. Don't look so disappointed."

"I'm not, I just think if we wait, chances of getting caught go up."

"Not necessarily."

"Whatever you say," she frowned. "You're the boss. I'm just the tied-up hostage."

Gavin glared sideways at her and ignored her. He revved up the engine and headed back toward the highway. At least he turned the lights on again. They were far enough away that the police couldn't see them anyway.

Snow was getting thicker and the winds were becoming gusty as they headed south back to town. It was well after midnight and Claire would be happy to find another motel and sleep. Maybe Gavin was right? Maybe everything would look better in the morning?

"Let's listen to some music?" she suggested, bending forward to switch it on with her zip-tied hands. "Could you do it for me please?"

Gavin shifted his jaw and turned on the radio without saying a word.

They caught the tail end of a news report: *"...if you've seen escaped child killer Gavin Parker Stevenson or Claire Bellefonte, please report it to the police immediately. Stevenson is considered armed and dangerous..."*

Click, Gavin switched it off mid-sentence. "I'm sick of hearing that."

"Me too."

As the Camaro headed down the dark snowy highway back to town, Claire considered the possibilities. She was out of cash with only her credit card left. She couldn't use that for the motel, so what were their options?

Leaning her head against the cool passenger window, she looked up at the falling snow. What was she doing with him anyway? Maybe all this was a mistake? If she told him she wanted out, he'd let her go. But observing his demeanor right now made her reconsider. His hope had depleted. His broad shoulders were slumped, and his unshaven face was fixed in a permanent frown.

How could she walk away now?

"Gavin," she turned to him, "don't give up!"

"You should talk."

His barbs flew back in her face, but she ignored them. Sighing, she tried again. "What if we do something totally different."

"And what would that be?"

"Surrender?"

"NO WAY!" Gavin was fuming now. "This *is my do or die, Claire!* Remember? You said it yourself. I surrender - I get a lethal injection! Got that? There is no *operation* for me. You don't get second chances on death row!"

Claire hung her head unsure of how to help him or what to say now. All she knew was they had run out of options and money. "What about an appeal?"

"I can't appeal, *not anymore!*"

With that, Gavin sped off into the night going well over the speed limit on slippery dangerous roads. Claire hoped his driving skills wouldn't be affected by his mood.

Suddenly, a vehicle burst onto the highway from the left approach and nearly sideswiped them. It was a police cruiser with flashing lights and sirens.

"Oh *no!*" she cried.

"*Crap!*"

The Camaro swerved, slip-sliding as Gavin tried to straighten it out. He pushed the gas pedal harder, trying to outrun the cop car, but nothing worked. The cruiser was right on their tail.

"*Go-go-go!*" she said.

Gavin revved through the gears.

Bang! The cruiser hit them from behind!

Then another cop car.

"*In front!*" she screamed.

But when Gavin turned to miss the vehicle, he lost control. The Camaro did a 360, hit the ditch, and flipped end over end. Everything went flying through the night, and the end had finally come.

Claire came too, hanging up-side-down from her seatbelt, still bound with zip-ties. Gavin must have been thrown from the vehicle. She couldn't find him and couldn't see past the curtain airbags which had deployed at her front and side. The car was filling with swamp water fast, and that made it hard to breathe with the mouthfuls she was taking in. A panic rose in her chest as someone reached in through the mayhem and started cutting her seatbelt free.

Was it Gavin? She couldn't tell.

Then, pulled from underwater, she felt someone dragging her wet frozen body to shore. "Gavin?"

"Shhh," the voice calmed. But that was the last thing he said. Shots rang out in the dark night and she heard a body fall.

*

Four days had passed since the accident. Claire didn't know what happened to Gavin until she saw it on the six o'clock news that night in the hospital with her leg in a cast: *"Escaped child killer Gavin Parker Stevenson came out of a medically induced coma today after police shot him Saturday during a high-speed chase near the border. Kidnapped Claire Bellefonte, was rescued from the scene and remains in hospital with non-life-threatening injuries. Bellefonte is expected to make a full recovery and will be released from hospital tomorrow when she'll make a formal statement to the media. Stevenson, given the death penalty for killing his wife and four children two years ago, is expected to return to death row as soon as possible. The court is pushing for his sentence to be expedited in lieu of the new kidnapping charges, and if that happens, Stevenson could be executed in as little as six months time."*

Claire felt sick to her stomach. "Gah!" she moaned, turning the TV off. She couldn't imagine what Gavin was going through right now. It didn't look like there was any hope for him. Still, surely something could be done. She could come clean and tell them he didn't really kidnap her. She could explain that she was a willing participant. *That she loved him.*

But somehow Claire knew that would sound ridiculous. No, Gavin was right. Her confession would only lead to charges, and she definitely didn't want to go to jail. It was a difficult situation, but Claire wanted to fix it somehow. According to the media, she was going to be giving them a statement soon, even though she'd already given one to the police. What could she say that would give Gavin a second chance without incriminating herself?

Nothing!

Claire sighed as she closed her eyes, wiping the tears that fell. Gavin was an extraordinary man and nobody knew it. They didn't know the pain he was suffering; They didn't know the loss he felt or the guilt he carried. They only saw the picture the media painted of him: *A child killer.*

It was horrible!

A child killer wouldn't have saved her life. He had many chances to kill her, but he didn't. Instead, he chose to drag her out of a submerged vehicle and save her life when he could have saved his own.

Why didn't he run?

Claire swallowed hard and realized she had to do something to return the favor.

By the next day, as she sat in her wheelchair in the hospital lobby, a rush of reporters flooded to her side when they saw her. It was to be expected, but still intimidating. Claire swallowed and fought off the panic, focusing on her one objective: to make them all see that Gavin was not the monster they thought he was.

"Miss Bellefonte?" the news broadcaster spoke. "Did you think Stevenson was going to kill you?"

"No, I did not!"

"Did you know he killed his own children with a butcher knife?"

Claire wanted to say that he didn't do it, but they wouldn't believe her anyway. She had to say something that would convince them he was innocent. "I felt very safe with Mr. Stevenson. I was shocked when I realized he was accused of killing his family. I seriously doubt he even did it. He's a very loving caring man and I'd like to see him get a new trial."

With that, the crowd became very noisy and she could hear some of them gasp.

"So, it's fair to say that he brainwashed you then?" the reporter continued to drill her.

"Absolutely not! I call it like I see it, and he was..."

"Miss Bellefonte, are you sympathizing with this man?" the reporter interrupted her. It seemed as if he was out to get her now.

"No - but I..."

"Then you understand he's facing the death penalty for what he's done?"

"Yes - but..."

"Miss Bellefonte, surely you don't condone what he's done?"

Claire was beyond annoyed now. She had to put a stop to this.

"I'm trying to tell you..."

"You're trying to tell us what?"

"Stop interrupting and let me finish!"

The room was hushed as they finally focused on what she had to stay.

"Gavin Parker Stevenson saved my life. I could have drowned in that vehicle but I didn't because he pulled me out. Why would he do that if he was a murderer? He could have saved his own butt, but he saved mine instead! Surely the courts will take this into consideration and give him a new trial. *Surely!*"

But then the microphone was pulled away from her mouth and the cameraman focused on only the reporter now. "And there you have it, folks. Miss Bellefonte has obviously suffered some trauma both physically and mentally. Apparently, victims of crime are sometimes confused in their relationship with their accusers, but I'm assured Miss Bellefonte will receive the best therapy the state has to offer. We're told Stevenson had her tied up, so the threat to her life *was* real whether she admits it or not. With the proper therapy, she should come to realize this, but experts say this may never happen."

Claire could feel her blood boil. She got whisked away and led to a car transporting her out of there as quickly as possible. The hired private nurse shushed her as they drove away from the hospital.

"That was an *ambush!*"

"Miss Bellefonte," the nurse said in a calming tone, "let's just focus on getting you well again."

What for? she wanted to say. Didn't they all know by now that she had her own death sentence? There was no getting better. But she didn't need to tell them that. They already questioned her sanity. Instead, Claire just kept silent and brushed her tears away as she thought of Gavin.

*

Over the next few months, Claire wrote several letters to Gavin Parker Stevenson as he awaited his expedited death sentence. They all returned unopened.

As winter turned to spring, and the snow began to melt, Claire remembered the first day it fell. The day she met *him*. Like the other men in her life that had come and gone, the sting of rejection lingered. But Gavin was different. Why? She didn't really know. Perhaps it was because of what he taught her about herself? He was the only one who cared enough to help her realize her value.

Then, one warm spring morning, she turned on the news and her heart skipped a beat when she saw his picture. It was Gavin - same ruggedly handsome face, same dark stubble chin, same tender blue eyes.

And she thought of the kiss.

Her heart pounded in her chest as the news reporter announced his execution day. Just two weeks from today. She wiped the tears that streamed down her face and started writing the last letter she'd ever write him. Maybe this one he'd open? On the back of the letter, she simply wrote: *Please?*

Two days before the execution, Claire received her letter back unopened again. But this time, she also received a small prisonissued postcard, and it was from him.

Dearest Claire,

I don't want to hurt you any more than I already have. All I want to say is I hope you live a long and happy healthy life and have a house full of babies and a wonderful husband who adores you. You deserve it double 'D' - now LIVE!

Claire wept like never before. Not only had he taught her how to love, but how to live. He was the only one who got her through the last six months, and he didn't even know it. That's what she told him in her letters had he bothered to open them. But maybe correspondence wasn't allowed, given the circumstances.

But she had to let him know somehow. They wouldn't let her visit him. They wouldn't let him speak to her on the phone, and tomorrow he would be gone. Quickly, she realized she had to take action. She made some calls and realized what she had to do.

She drove to the penitentiary the next day and got there well ahead of schedule, knowing exactly how she was going to repay him for what he gave her. And thankfully they allowed her to sit with other guests who wanted to be there to witness the execution. She was warned that prisoners weren't allowed to speak or say any last goodbyes. She was somehow okay with that.

What she had planned would make up for it anyway.

As Claire found her seat in the stuffy observation room with only glass separating her from a bed where they were to administer the lethal injection, she looked around at who else was there. Angry eyes glared back at her from every seat.

That was okay, she decided. Her eyes would love him.

And when the time came, she started to tremble. They brought Gavin in looking the same as she remembered him. His big muscular arms were exposed like the day she picked him up. She wanted to call out to him but knew he couldn't hear her anyway. He was positioned in such a way so he could see everyone, and his fear was unmistakable. Claire wished it didn't have to be this way. The angry people across from her pointed fingers of accusation at him and screamed insults through the glass.

And now it was her turn.

Without warning, she stood up in her seat and made Gavin notice. He immediately recognized her. With a wide smile and tears tumbling from her eyes, she took off her jacket, exposing a pink breast cancer t-shirt with the letters 'DD' on the front.

Gavin cocked his head immediately.

She patted her flat chest and bit her lip, telling him without words what she had done. Tears continued to gush as she mouthed a *thank you* to him, and blew a final kiss goodbye. His eyes suddenly lost their fear as he threw his head back and gave a heaving sigh of relief. He nodded to her, then breathed in his last breath with a smile.

Claire lived cancer free for the rest of her life after that. And when she gave birth to her first son, she told her husband there was only one name she'd consider.

Gavin!

THE END

To read more from Kathleen Morris, please go to her author page on Amazon.com.